For my Mum, Mary Patricia Elverson,
for always being there and being my inspiration.

Away

Written by Dani Seatter

Illustrated by Anna Stead

Rabbit *hopped,* stopped, looked,

"Hmm," Rabbit said.

Deer trotted, stopped, gazed,

"What's that?" Deer said.

Rabbit looked puzzled.

Deer looked *perplexed.*

"It's a hat," said Deer,

"It's a top," said Rabbit.

Mouse scurried, stopped, stared,

"Oh," Mouse squeaked.

Butterfly fluttered, stopped, peered,

"Weird," Butterfly cried!

Mouse appeared confused.

Butterfly appeared amused.

"It's a house," proclaimed Mouse,

"It's a cloud," explained Butterfly.

Fox galloped, stopped, gaped,

"Well," Fox snorted.

Squirrel s c u t t l e d, stopped, studied,

"That's swell," Squirrel said.

Fox seemed worried.

Squirrel seemed interested.

"It's a pillow?" said Fox,

"It's a den," said Squirrel.

Bee, b u z z e d, stopped, watched,

"Gosh," whispered Bee.

Robin f l u r r i e d, stopped, gawped,

"Ooh," chirped Robin.

Bee seemed concerned.

Robin seemed impressed.

"It's a trap," said Bee,

"It's a nest," said Robin.

Owl flapped, stopped, considered,

"Why?" shouted Owl.

Badger am b l e d , stopped, goggled,

"Who?" Badger growled.

Owl looked cross.

Badger looked annoyed.

"It's plastic," snapped Owl,

"It's rubbish," exclaimed Badger.

"What do we do with it?" they asked.

"Throw it away," said Badger,

"Where?" questioned Owl.

They looked around,

There was no 'away.'

"Oh," they said softly.

"I'll use it first," said Rabbit,

"And I'll use it after," said Deer.

"Then me," squeaked Bee,

"And me," exclaimed Squirrel.

Then Owl flapped a wing,

there was another something

r o l l i n g, r a t t l i n g, in the breeze.

It stopped at Fox's feet.

"Oh," they all said.

Published by Eco-Able Ltd 2021. ISBN 978-1-9196003-0-7

www.eco-able.co.uk